Ladybird Readers

The Story of Laila and Ajeet

Series Editor: Sorrel Pitts
Text adapted by Mandeep Locham
Illustrated by Kamala Nair
Song lyrics by Naomi Rainbow

LADYBIRD BOOKS

UK | USA | Canada | Ireland | Australia
India | New Zealand | South Africa

Ladybird Books is part of the Penguin Random House group of companies
whose addresses can be found at global.penguinrandomhouse.com.
www.penguin.co.uk   www.puffin.co.uk   www.ladybird.co.uk

Penguin
Random House
UK

Text adapted from *Tales from India* by Bali Rai, first published by Puffin Books, 2017
This Ladybird Readers version first published by Ladybird Books Ltd, 2022
001

Original copyright © Bali Rai, 2017
Text copyright © Ladybird Books Ltd, 2022
Illustrations copyright © Ladybird Books Ltd, 2022

Printed in Italy

The authorized representative in the EEA is Penguin Random House Ireland,
Morrison Chambers, 32 Nassau Street, Dublin D02 YH68

A CIP catalogue record for this book is available from the British Library

ISBN: 978–0–241–53364–2

All correspondence to:
Ladybird Books
Penguin Random House Children's
One Embassy Gardens, 8 Viaduct Gardens, London SW11 7BW

Ladybird 🐞 Readers

The Story of Laila and Ajeet

Adapted from *Tales From India*
by Bali Rai

Picture words

Prince Ajeet

Princess Laila

Mother and Father

the terrible Rajah

parrot

ant

tigers

monsters

bow and arrow

shoot

fall in love

seeds

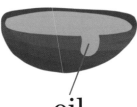

oil

axe

rope / tie

Prince Ajeet lived with his mother and father. He loved the forest that was near his home. He went there every day.

One day, Ajeet went into the forest with his horse. They ran past a tree with parrots in it. The parrots were frightened!

Ajeet stopped his horse. "I'm sorry I frightened you," he said to the parrots.

"I am the Parrot King—the pet of Princess Laila," the Parrot King said. "I will tell her that you were nice to us."

"Who is Princess Laila?" Ajeet asked.

"Laila is as lovely as the sun and the moon," the Parrot King said. "Laila is kind and clever, but her father is the terrible Rajah. If you fall in love with her, he will give you a very hard job to do. If you cannot do it, he will kill you!"

When Prince Ajeet went home,
he was sad for six days and six
nights. He told his parents about
Princess Laila and the terrible Rajah.

Ajeet's mother and father were very worried. But Ajeet knew that he had to find the princess.

"I want to help her," said Ajeet. He left on his horse to find her.

When Ajeet stopped to eat, there were ants all over his food! "These ants are hungry, too!" he thought. Ajeet laughed. He gave them his food.

"I am the Ant Queen," the biggest ant said. "Thank you! If you ever need help, we will come!"

That night, Ajeet heard loud, frightening noises.

He saw two tigers through the trees.

One tiger said "I've got something in my foot and it really hurts!"

"I can help you," said Ajeet.

"Thank you!" said the tiger.
"If you ever need help, we will come!"

The next day, Ajeet saw an old man on the road. He was carrying a heavy bag.

"I can help you," said Ajeet.

"Thank you," said the old man. "My bag is magic—if you want something, think of it, and it will be in the bag!"

Suddenly, two men jumped out.

They took Ajeet's horse—but they BOTH wanted it!

Ajeet thought of a bow and arrow.
He looked in the bag, and they
were there!

"The man who brings back this
arrow can have my horse," he said.

Ajeet shot the arrow far away.
The two men ran to find it.

"Take my horse, quick," Ajeet said to the old man, "before they come back. I can walk."

"Thank you," said the old man. "You are so kind. Here, please take my magic bag."

Later, Ajeet became tired
from walking. He thought of a
flying bed. He looked in the bag,
and one was there!

"Take me to Princess Laila!"
Ajeet said. The bed took him from
east to west through sun and rain.

The bed stopped by Princess Laila's window. She was singing a sad song about a bird that could not fly.

"I will make Princess Laila's sad song happy," Ajeet thought.

Every night, Ajeet took a present to Princess Laila while she slept and left it at her window.

One morning, Laila opened her eyes while Ajeet was leaving.

"Why do you leave me presents?" she asked.

"To win your love," Ajeet said.

Every evening, Ajeet and Laila talked. They soon fell in love.

The princess spoke to her mother.

Then, together they went to
the Rajah.

He was very angry and sent his men
to find Prince Ajeet.

"If you want to marry my daughter, you must do a job for me. If you cannot do it, you will be killed," the Rajah shouted.

The Rajah took Ajeet to a field.

"When I come back, a hundred bowls must be full with oil from these seeds," said the Rajah, and he laughed.

Ajeet had an idea. He called for
the ants . . .

. . . and they came!

"We will help you," the Ant Queen
said. The ants found the seeds and
broke them into the bowls.
Soon, the bowls were full of oil.

When the Rajah came back, he was very angry.

"I will give you ANOTHER job!" he said.

"There are two monsters behind this door," the Rajah said. "If you fight them and win, you can ask the princess to marry you."

Again, Ajeet had an idea.

He called for the tigers . . .

. . . and they came!

Ajeet opened the door.

The monsters saw the tigers
and began to cry.

"Do you really want to fight?"
the tigers asked.

"Please don't kill us. We only want
to go home," said the monsters.

"Go!" said Ajeet, and the monsters ran out of the room.

"What?!" screamed the Rajah.
"Where are my monsters?
Prince Ajeet, tomorrow you will die!"

Princess Laila was sad. She did not sleep that night. She planned to help Ajeet.

The next morning, Ajeet was tied
with ropes and brought to the Rajah.

"Kill him!" the Rajah shouted. The Rajah's man threw an axe at Ajeet.

The ropes were too strong. The axe could not cut them.

The Rajah was very angry.

"Take him away!" he shouted.

"No, take HIM away!" Princess Laila shouted back. She pointed to her father. "You are a terrible father! You are a terrible, horrible Rajah!"

The people saw that Princess Laila's hair was very short! The strong ropes were made from her hair. They stopped the axe, and saved Prince Ajeet.

Prince Ajeet and Princess Laila married.

They were all very happy, and the people were happy because they had a kind and clever prince and princess.

Laila and Ajeet were happy for many years.

Activities

The key below describes the skills practiced in each activity.

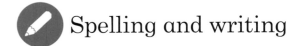 Spelling and writing

Reading

Speaking

Listening*

Critical thinking

Singing*

Preparation for the Cambridge
Young Learners exams

*To complete these activities, listen to the audio downloads
available at www.ladybirdeducation.co.uk

1 Match the words to the pictures.

1 Prince Ajeet

    a

2 Princess Laila

    b

3 terrible Rajah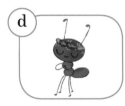

    c

4 Parrot King

    d

5 tigers

    e

6 Ant Queen

    f

2 Find the words.

m	u	m	o	n	s	t	e	r	s	w	y
b	l	z	f	z	l	f	h	o	x	t	a
o	y	n	d	t	s	i	u	p	e	b	r
t	g	q	b	e	h	n	s	e	e	d	s
i	c	f	t	s	r	p	n	l	g	a	o
g	x	m	h	h	c	e	e	l	p	d	a
p	a	r	r	o	t	s	g	h	s	r	x
c	t	b	e	o	m	c	j	m	t	l	e
z	w	s	n	t	i	g	e	r	s	y	t
n	b	t	h	r	t	m	r	s	w	f	f
a	o	i	l	h	g	s	o	i	a	z	z
s	a	e	u	g	b	q	a	b	m	g	b

monsters

shoot

rope

axe

seeds

oil

parrots

tigers

3 **Find the words.**

prince
mother
father
forest
home

lprince
hyforesthjlmotherkprhomeyndrafatherqw

4 Ask and answer the questions with a friend. 🗨 ❓

1 Where was Ajeet?

He was in the forest.

2 Was Ajeet with his horse?

3 What was in the tree?

4 Was Ajeet frightened?

5 **Read the text. Choose the correct words and write them next to 1—5.**

lovely   cannot   fall   terrible   job

"Laila is as ¹ __lovely__ as the sun and the moon," the Parrot King said. "Laila is kind and clever, but her father is the ² _____ Rajah. If you ³ _____ in love with her, he will give you a very hard

⁴ _____ to do. If you

⁵ _____ do it, he will kill you!"

6 **Match the two parts of the sentences. Then, write them on the lines.**

1 When Ajeet stopped to eat,

2 "These ants

3 "If you ever need help,

a are hungry too!"

b we will come."

c there were ants all over his food!

1 When Ajeet stopped to eat, there were ants all over his food!

2 ....

....

3 ....

....

7 Write about this story.

8 Order the story. Write 1—5.

.... Ajeet thought of a bow and arrow. He looked in the bag, and they were there!

___1___ Suddenly, two men jumped out. They took Ajeet's horse—but they BOTH wanted it!

.... "Take my horse, quick," Ajeet said to the old man, "before they come back."

.... "The man who brings back this arrow can have my horse," he said.

.... "You are so kind," said the old man. "Here, please take my magic bag."

9 Write the correct form of the verbs. 📖 ✏️

The bed ....._stopped_..... **(stop)** by Princess Laila's window. She was singing a sad song about a bird that .... **(can)** not fly.

"I will make Princess Laila's sad song happy," Ajeet .... **(think)**. Every night, Ajeet took a present to Princess Laila and .... **(leave)** it at her window.

One morning, Laila opened her eyes while Ajeet was .... **(leave)**.

10 Do the crossword.

Down

1 Ajeet loved the . . . that was near his home.

3 Laila was kind and . . .

Across

2 Ajeet thought of a . . . and arrow.

4 Laila's father was the . . . Rajah.

5 Ajeet and Laila soon fell in . . .

11 Look and read. Write the answers as complete sentences.

1 Where was Ajeet?

   He was in a field   .

2 Who was helping Ajeet?

   ....

3 What were the bowls full of?

   ....

12 Who said this?

Ajeet

Laila

the Rajah

1 "Take me to Princess Laila!"

said _____Ajeet_____.

2 "Why do you leave me presents?"

asked _____.

3 "To win your love,"

said _____.

4 "You must do a job for me,"

said _____.

5 "Tomorrow you will die!"

said _____.

13 Read the answers.
Write the questions.

1 Who did Ajeet call for?

He called for the tigers.

2 How many monsters ....

....?

There were two.

3 Why ....

....?

Because they wanted to go home.

14 **Listen, and** ✓ **the boxes.**

1 Who was worried?

(a)  ✓

(b)

(c)

2 Who was frightened?

(a)

(b)

(c)

3 Who was sad?

(a)

(b)

(c)

4 Who was tired?

(a)

(b)

(c)

15 Look at the pictures.
Tell the story to your friend. 🗨 ✦

1

2

3

4

5

6

*Princess Laila was sad,
and she could not sleep . . .*

16 **Listen, and write the answers.**

1 Who did the girl like in the story?

Princess Laila

2 Why did she like Laila?

3 What did Ajeet find in the magic bag?

4 Which animal did the girl like best?

5 Which animals helped Ajeet?

17 Sing the song. 🎵

Prince Ajeet met the Parrot King,
the pet of Princess Laila.
Her father was the terrible Rajah.
Ajeet wanted to help her!

Prince Ajeet helped the ants,
he gave them his food.
He helped the tigers,
And the old man too.

Here is Princess Laila!
Why is she so sad?
The Rajah gave Ajeet a hard job to do.
It was very bad . . .

But the ants helped Prince Ajeet,
And the tigers helped him too,
"Take him away!" shouted the Rajah.
"No!" said Laila. "They should take you!"

Ajeet and Laila were kind and clever,
And they were happy together!

Visit **www.ladybirdeducation.co.uk**
for more FREE Ladybird Readers resources

✓ Digital edition of every title
✓ Audio tracks (US/UK)
✓ Answer keys
✓ Lesson plans

✓ Role-plays
✓ Classroom display material
✓ Flashcards
✓ User guides

Register and sign up to the newsletter to receive your FREE classroom resource pack!

To access the audio and digital versions of this book:

1 Go to **www.ladybirdeducation.co.uk**
2 Click "Unlock book"
3 Enter the code below

S43cjjKcI1